FIELD MOUSE GOES TO WAR

by Edward A. Kennard

Illustrated by Fred Kabotie

Kiva Publishing • Walnut, California

Library of Congress Cataloging-in-Publication Data

Kennard, Edward A. (Edward Allan), 1907–
    Field mouse goes to war / by Edward A. Kennard; illustrated by Fred Kabotie.
       p. cm.
    Originally published: [Washington] : Education Division, U.S. Indian Service, [1944].
    Summary: A little field mouse helps his human neighbors, the Mishongnovi, by killing
a marauding hawk that is preying on their chickens.
    ISBN 1-885772-19-X (paperback)
    1. Hopi Indians—Folklore. 2. Tales—Arizona. [1. Hopi Indians—Folklore. 2. Indians of
North America—Arizona—Folklore. 3. Folklore—Arizona.] I. Kabotie, Fred, ill. II. Title.

E99.H7 K44 2000
398.24'529353'0899745—dc21   99-089875

Design by Ali Graphics Services Inc.
Printed in USA
9 8 7 6 5 4 3 2 1

Kiva Publishing, Walnut, CA

INTRODUCTION

During the 1940's, the Bureau of Indian Affairs took a fresh look at literacy for Native Americans, especially in New Mexico and northern Arizona. They commissioned children's stories and poems, from pre-primer to middle reader levels, working with established authors and Indian artists. Some of the original books were bilingual, while others presented their stories entirely in English.

This book is one of several works from this series selected for today's young readers. Literacy is still extremely important, and so is understanding the cultures of indigenous peoples. A new presentation of these stories is therefore appropriate for a much broader population than the one for which they were originally intended.

From an educational standpoint, they are authentic representations of a unique culture in a simpler time. The stories are told with sincerity and directness. The illustrations, by the foremost artists from the early years of Indian watercolor painting, portray the elegance and harmony of that world. Even today these traditional tales continue to evoke wonder, interest, and satisfaction.

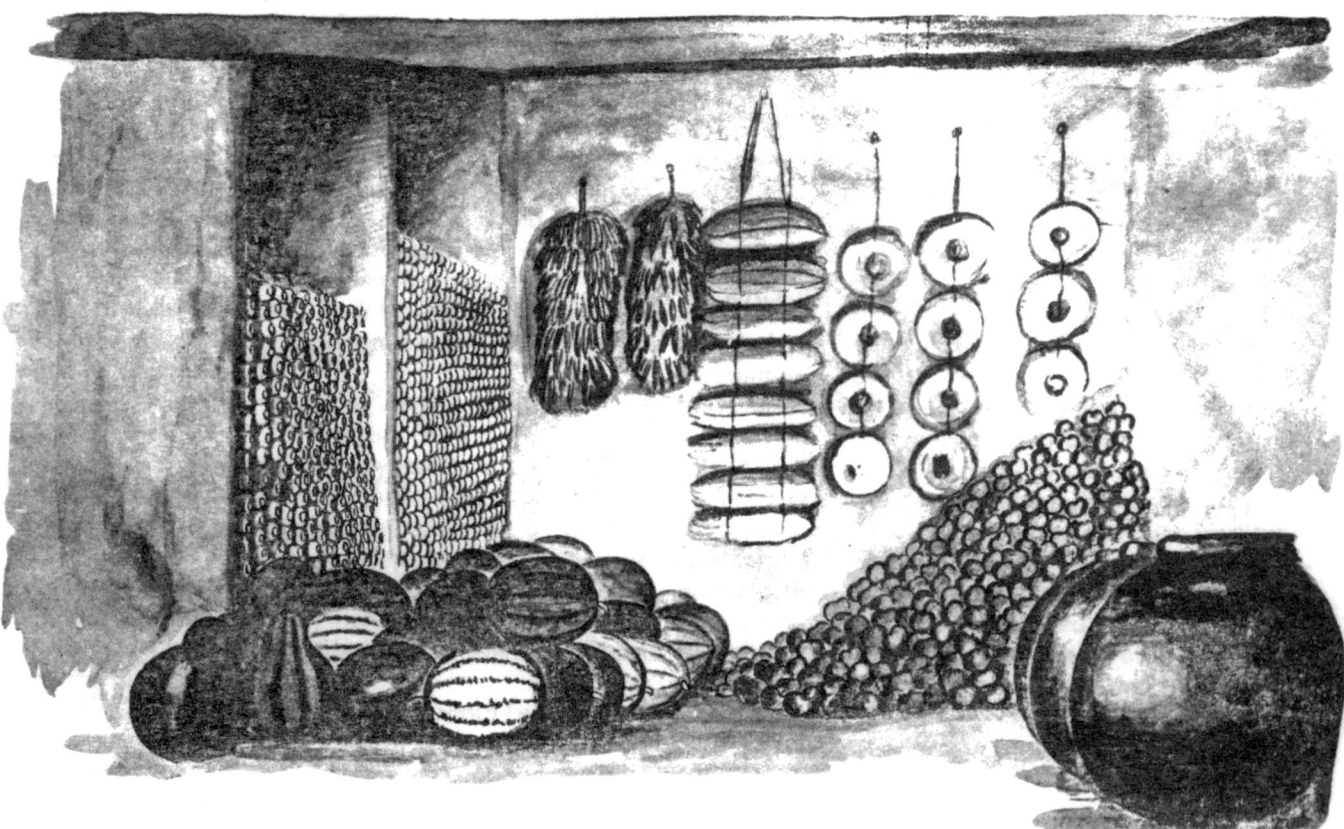

MOST STORIES happened long ago and far away.
But this story is different.
This story happened right at Mishongnovi
    and it was not so very long ago.
At that time the Mishongnovi people were very rich.

Their storerooms were filled with corn and
    beans and squash and melons.
They had peaches and apples and apricots.
They had many sheep and many goats
    and many horses and many cattle.
They even had burros.
Of course, they had always had corn and beans
    and squash from the very Beginning.

They had had peaches, apples, and apricots for so
    long that they believed they had always had them.
The old men could even tell a story to prove it.

But their proudest possessions were their chickens.
Chickens were new.

Old people remembered when they first came.
But they were very proud of them even if they were new.
Year after year there were more and more chickens—for a while.

Then things changed.

They began to lose their chickens.
They had a hard time.
At least, that is what they said.
Of course they had plenty of everything else.
So, they ate and ate and became fatter and fatter.

But to hear them talk anyone would think they were going
    to starve the very next day if they lost one more chicken.

On top of Corn Rock lived a hawk.
This hawk was the great enemy of the
    Mishongnovi people.
He was the one who was killing their chickens.
Day after day he killed more and more chickens.
Day after day the chickens that were left
    became fewer and fewer.
In a little while there would be no chickens at all.

The people were worried.
The people were troubled.
All they talked about was that hawk who
    was killing their chickens.

The boys were always making plans to kill the hawk.
But nothing came of their plans and the chickens
    were killed just the same as before.
The women told one another how many
    chickens they had lost.
They told one another how scarce eggs were.

They told their husbands and fathers and nephews
    and sons to kill the hawk.
The men agreed.
They knew it was up to them.
They had meetings.
They went to the kivas and they talked all night.

They talked all night for many nights.
They made plans, too.
But they did not kill the hawk.

The Village Chief and the Crier had a meeting.
They knew that their people were troubled.
They smoked and talked and prayed.
Something had to be done.

They smoked and talked and prayed some more.
They knew what had to be done.
The hawk had to be killed.

Everyone knew that.

The men and women and boys knew it.
Even the children knew
But no one knew how.

A little field mouse lived on the south side of the village.
He heard all about all the trouble the Mishongnovi
    people were having.
He felt very sorry for them.
He felt so sorry that he decided to kill the hawk for them.

One night he picked up his tobacco pouch and went
    to the house of the Village Chief.
He knocked on the door.
"Come in," they called.
He went in.

The Village Chief was surprised to see him.
"Sit down there.
Eat," he told the mouse.
The mouse sat down and ate a meal of corn
    mush and boiled beans.

When he had eaten enough he moved away from
    the bowls of food and sat against the wall.
Finally the Village Chief said, "I guess you had
    some reason for coming here."
"Yes," said the field mouse.
"But wait until we have a smoke first."

The field mouse took out his tobacco pouch.
He took out his pipe.

He filled the pipe and lighted it.
He smoked and offered it to the Village Chief.
The Chief smoked a while and passed it back.
When they had finished smoking, the Chief asked again,
    "Why have you come here?"
Then the mouse told him, "I feel very sorry
    for you and your people.
I pity you because this hawk is killing all your chickens."

The Village Chief said, "Is that so?
What do you plan to do about it?"
"I have been thinking about it.
I shall try to do something for you.
I shall try to kill the hawk for you."

The Village Chief just looked at the little mouse.
In his heart he was thinking,
 "This little mouse cannot do anything.
He is too small.
Surely he cannot kill that hawk.
After all, the Crier and I don't know how.
The men don't know how.
The boys have failed."
But he did not say that to the mouse.
Instead, he said, "All right. Thank you."

Then the mouse told him, "Tomorrow you will announce it.
The time will come in four days.
Until that time the women can be getting ready.

The third day will be *totokya*—
    the day of preparation—and the
    fourth day will be the dance day.
Then I shall kill this enemy.
So, having these thoughts in mind, we shall approach that day."

The Village Chief was happy.
The little mouse spoke just right.
Maybe he could kill their enemy.
He told the mouse, "Tomorrow morning
    the Crier will announce it."
"All right. We'll go to sleep," the mouse said.

He picked up his pipe and his tobacco bag and went home.

After the mouse had gone,
    the Chief picked up his tobacco bag and pipe
    and went to the Crier's house.
He knocked on the door.
"Come in," he was told.
When he went inside they offered him food,
    but he ate only a little.
He was too excited to eat much.
He filled his pipe.
He lit it and smoked four times.

He passed the pipe to the Crier.
The Crier took it, saying, "My father."
The Crier smoked four times and passed it back.

The Kikmongwi said, "My father,
I think we have done our part with this smoke.
Now why have you come?"
The Village Chief answered, "I have
    come because of the trouble we are having.
You know what that trouble is.
Tonight I had a visitor.
This visitor offered his help.

He set a date.
He told me to have you announce that the great
    event will take place in four days.
The third day will be totokya and the fourth day
    will be the dance day.
On that day he will kill our enemy.
So with happy hearts let us prepare for that day."

The Crier asked,
    "Who is the one who will help us?"
"It is that dirty little field mouse who lives
    on the south side of the village."
At first the Crier wanted to laugh.
Then he was angry.
Next he wondered if the Chief had lost his mind.

Finally, he said, "All right.
    I will give the message to our children."
There was nothing else he could say.
There was nothing else he could do.
Then the Crier filled and lit his pipe and
    offered it to the Chief who said, "My child."
The Chief smoked four times and passed back the
    pipe to the Crier who said "My father."

The Crier smoked four times.
When he had finished the Chief said,
    "Thinking only of this great
        event, let us go to sleep."
The Village Chief went home.
He went to bed.

But the Crier stayed up all night.
Four times he went out and looked at the stars.
The fourth time was just before sunrise.
Then he made the announcement
    from the housetop.

The little mouse heard it and was happy.
The people heard it and laughed.

The first day the men went far to the
    north to bring back wood.
The women shelled corn.
All day they laughed at the little mouse.
They told one another he was
    too small to kill the hawk.

They said he could not succeed when they
    themselves had failed.
The second day the men hauled water from
    springs far below the village.
The women ground corn all day long.
The second day they were angry.
They were angry at the mouse and the
    Village Chief and the Crier.

They said that the dirty little mouse was
    crazy to even try to kill the hawk.
They said that the Village Chief was crazy
    to even listen to the mouse.
They said that the Crier was crazy to set the date.
They said all their hard work would be for nothing.

The third day was *totokya*.
The men butchered sheep.

They killed many sheep.
The women made *piki* and *pik'ami*, too.
They worked all day long.
It was a great day of preparation.

The third day they wondered.
They wondered if the mouse had some great power.
They wondered if the Chief knew the mouse had power.

They told one another it could not be helped.
It had been decided.
It had been announced.
They would have to do their part.

On *totokya* the little mouse was getting ready, too.

He took a greasewood stick.
With his knife he sharpened it to a point.
He made the point very sharp.

From inside his kiva he dug a hole under the ground
    that came out quite a distance from his kiva.
That night when everyone in the village went to
    sleep the little mouse stayed up all night long.
He smoked all night.

Three times he went out and looked at the stars.
The third time when he came back he took out his feathers
    and his war paints and other things.
He began to dress himself.
On top of his head he tied the tip of a feather from an eagle's
    wing with a downy feather from an eagle's breast.
He tied them with cotton.

With white clay he painted his cheeks and
    the right side of his forehead.
He put the white on his arms and chest and
    on his thighs and legs.
He painted a black mark across his eyes.
He put on his kilt.
He tied shells from the ocean around his right wrist.
He got his bow and his war club.

He took off his moccasins.
Then he sat down and thought about his songs.
Dressed like a real warrior, he thought like a real warrior.
The next day was the great event.
The next day was the dance day.

All the Mishongnovi people got up early and
    washed their heads.
They dressed their children in their newest clothes.
The men wore their brightest headbands, their silver belts,
    and their turquoise necklaces.
The women wore their bracelets and rings of silver and
    turquoise and their brightest shawls.
Visitors came from all the other villages.
They came on horseback, on burros, in wagons, and on foot.
They were all dressed up, too.

They came to see their friends and relations.
They came to talk and to joke.
They came to eat *piki* and *pik'ami*, *somiviki* and *noqkwivi*.
Boys came to smile at the girls.
But most of all they came to see the dance.
Everyone wondered what was going to happen.

Some laughed.
They said the little mouse was too small to kill the hawk.
Others were angry.
They said it was foolish to set the date and have the
    dance and do all the work for nothing.
They said the visitors were laughing at them.

But a few did not laugh
    and they were not angry.
They said, "Wait and see.
Maybe that mouse has some great power."

By noon there was a big crowd.
They all gathered around the little mouse's kiva.
The people were surprised.

Tied to the ladder was a real warrior's standard.
It was a bow standard.
It looked like it was going to be a war dance.
Just at noon the little mouse came out.

He danced right in front of his kiva.
He danced all by himself.
He was dressed just like a real warrior.
The people laughed at him.

As he danced he sang this song.
"The hawk kills chickens.
The hawk kills rabbits.
But the hawk won't kill *Tusan Homichi*.
Monster Hawk will surely die."

The hawk was watching from the top of Corn Rock.
When he heard the song he became angry.
Just as he stretched his wings to fly down, the
    little mouse went back into his kiva.

The little mouse came out again.
This time he danced farther away from his kiva.
He sang his song again.
But all the time he sang and danced, he watched the hawk.
As he danced he went closer and closer to
    the opening of his kiva.
This time the hawk flew away from Corn Rock.
But the little mouse quickly ducked into his kiva
    and the hawk flew back.

The third time the little mouse came out he
    walked still farther away from his kiva.
He began to dance there.
He sang his song.
But as he danced he came closer and closer to his kiva.

This time the hawk swooped down, but just as he was
    about to catch him the mouse ducked into his kiva.
The people gasped.
They were frightened.
They were sure the hawk was going to kill him.
They told one another,
    "If that dirty little mouse does not stay close to
    his hole, the hawk will surely kill him next time."

Down in his kiva the little mouse was very busy.

He took his stick, his sharp-pointed greasewood stick,
    and crawled along the hole he had dug.

When he came to the opening he pushed
    up the stick so the sharp point stood up
    right next to the hole.
Then he crawled back to his kiva.
He came out again.
He walked far away from his kiva.
When he came to the other hole next to
    the pointed stick. he stopped.
He began to dance there.

The people were surprised.
The mouse was so foolish.
He was too far away.
It was just what they expected.

But they watched him dance, anyway.
This is what the little mouse sang while he danced,
"*Tusan Homichi, Tusan Homichi,*
    He has whiskers sticking from his nose."
Then he gave his war cry.

It sounded just like a mouse squeak,
    but it was his war cry, anyhow.
As he danced he lifted the bow in his left hand, and he lifted
    his war club in his right hand each time he turned around.

Then he sang, "The hawk kills chickens.
The hawk kills rabbits.
But the hawk won't kill Tusan Homichi.
Monster Hawk will surely die."

The hawk became very angry.
But he was sure he would kill the mouse this time.
He was too far away from his kiva.
When the little mouse finished his song,
    he shook his war club up at the hawk
    and just stood there.

The hawk swooped down from his high perch
    straight for the mouse.
Just as he reached him the little mouse jumped into the hole.

The hawk did not see the sharp-pointed stick.
He landed right on it and cut open his throat.
He rolled over dead.

That is how the little mouse got rid of
    the monster for the people.

At first the people could not believe their own eyes.
Then they were happy.

The Village Chief came down to the mouse's kiva.
The Crier came with him.
They both wore kilts and had their hair
    hanging loose down their backs.

While the little mouse stood in front of his kiva,
    the Chief and the Crier gave him prayer sticks
    and prayer feathers and sacred corn meal.

Then the Chief smoked over him and the Crier
    sprinkled him with medicine.
Then all the women of Mishongnovi started for his kiva.
The old women, the young women, and the girls
    all started down to the mouse's kiva.
They made a long line, and each had
    something on her back.

At his kiva the women gave him *piki* and
    pik'ami, *somiviki* and *noqkwivi*, and
    many other kinds of food.
They piled it all around his kiva.
That is how they paid him for his courage
    and his cleverness in killing the hawk.

About the Author and Illustrator

Edward A. Kennard collaborated with Hopi storyteller Albert Yava to create this story as part of a literacy project for the Department of Education, Bureau of Indian Affairs in 1944. Contact Kiva Publishing for information on the availability of a bilingual edition.

Hopi artist Fred Kabotie (1900-1986) began his artistic career by illustrating *Taytay's Memories*, a book of stories by Elizabeth DeHuff. He continued to illustrate books and stories throughout his illustrious career, which included commissions from the Heye Foundation, the Fred Harvey Company, and the Indian Arts and Crafts Board; a Guggenheim Fellowship; teaching painting in the Hopi schools; and directing the Hopi Arts and Crafts Guild. He is generally regarded as the dean of early Southwestern Indian painting.